YEARLING BOOKS are designed especially to entertain and enlighten young people. Patricia Reilly Giff, consultant to this series, received her bachelor's degree from Marymount College and a master's degree in history from St. John's University. She holds a Professional Diploma in Reading and a Doctorate of Humane Letters from Hofstra University. She was a teacher and reading consultant for many years, and is the author of numerous books for young readers.

Molly
for Mayor
Judy Delton

Illustrated by Alan Tiegreen

A YEARLING BOOK

Published by
Bantam Doubleday Dell Books for Young Readers
a division of
Random House, Inc.
1540 Broadway
New York, New York 10036

Visit us on the Web! www.randomhouse.com

Educators and librarians, for a variety of teaching tools, visit us at www.randomhouse.com/teachers

ISBN: 0-440-41525-X

Printed in the United States of America

December 1999

10 9 8 7 6 5 4 3 2 1

CWO

Contents

For Tienne Otteson, my dear friend
and number one choice for mayor.

CHAPTER 1

Red Leaves, New Books, New Badges

"Fall is my favorite season," said Molly Duff, picking up some red maple leaves that had fluttered to the ground.

"It's called autumn," said Rachel Meyers. "That's the real name for it."

"Whatever it's called, it's not my favorite season," scoffed Sonny Stone. "I don't like any season that means school starts, that's for sure. July is my favorite season.

1

It's my birthday and we go to the lake and there's no school at all."

"July isn't a season. It's a month," said Mary Beth Kelly, who was Molly's best friend.

"I love a new school year!" said Rachel. "I get new clothes and books and pencils and tablets. My mom and I are going shopping at the Mall of America next Saturday."

Rachel had very nice clothes, thought Molly. Her father was a dentist and people said they were rich. Most of the Pee Wees agreed that she was the best-dressed Pee Wee Scout.

It was Tuesday, and the Scouts were on the way to their meeting at Mrs. Peters's house. She was their leader. There were thirteen Pee Wees altogether. They earned badges and learned new things, but mostly they had a good time. They had

2

treats every week, talked about their good deeds, sang the Pee Wee Scout song, and said the Pee Wee Scout pledge.

"Wheee!" shouted Roger White. "Geronimo!" He threw himself into a pile of leaves in someone's front yard. The pile scattered and blew away. Most of the leaves stuck to Roger's sweater.

"Hey, I'm a leaf guy!" he shouted.

"He's got a leaf brain," muttered Mary Beth.

"Now those people will have to rake all those leaves up again!" said Tracy Barnes. Then she sneezed. She was allergic to leaf mold.

A man came out and shook his fist at Roger, but he had run to the next block by that time. Roger was not Molly's favorite Pee Wee Scout.

By the time everyone caught up to Roger, he was busy drawing a mustache on a big sign on someone else's front lawn. The sign said VOTE FOR CLIFF NELSON FOR COUNCILMAN.

"What's a councilman?" Sonny asked.

"How could you not know that?" asked Rachel with a sigh.

But she didn't answer his question. No one else did either. Molly thought Kevin Moe would know about councilmen because he was so smart. He was going to be mayor someday. Maybe even president. Molly wanted to marry Kevin. Unless she married Jody George. Jody was smart too, and nice, and he had a wheelchair. No other Pee Wee had a wheelchair. Sometimes Jody let them ride in it.

But Kevin wasn't there, so no one answered the question.

"How come these signs are up all over the place?" asked Tracy.

That was an easy question. Even Molly knew that.

"It's because it's election time," she said. "These people want to be mayor or governor or president or something. The signs are campaign posters."

Now Roger was drawing glasses on Cliff. And a beard.

"You're defacing public property," said Rachel. "That's against the law. You could go to jail."

That was where Roger would end up, thought Molly. He was always doing something none of the other Pee Wees would do. Molly's mother said he was always looking for trouble.

Roger was drawing earrings on Cliff now. And a hat with a feather on it. And a pipe in his mouth.

"That guy won't like for people to think

he smokes," said Lisa Ronning. "That's a bad image for a public servant."

"Smoking's not so bad," said Sonny, pretending to puff on a pencil.

"It's bad enough to make you die," said Lisa.

Sonny put his hand on his chest and fell over on the sidewalk. Roger laughed and fell over too.

"They won't be laughing when their lungs get all black and icky," said Lisa.

"Everyone has these posters up in their yards," said Mary Beth. "I wouldn't know who to vote for even if I could vote."

Molly wasn't worried about voting. It would be a long, long time before the Pee Wees could vote.

"What badge do you think we'll work on next?" Molly asked Mary Beth.

"I don't know, but we should find out today," she answered.

"I hope it's a good one," said Lisa. "Like horseback riding or surfing or skydiving."

"I hope it's not something we have to learn, like bike rules again," said Roger.

Roger was the one who needed those rules the most, thought Molly.

The Pee Wees turned the corner and came to Mrs. Peters's house. Mrs. Peters stood on her front steps waving to them. Jody was wheeling up in his wheelchair, and Kevin and Patty and Kenny Baker were there too. So was Tim Noon.

Well, it won't be long now till we hear all about our new badge, thought Molly. The Scouts ran up their leader's front steps, walked politely through the house, and went down the basement steps to their meeting room. They took their places around the big table and waited for the meeting to begin. In a few minutes Molly would know what badge they would earn! She hoped it wasn't skydiving! She was afraid of heights. But rat's knees! Any badge would be fun if the Pee Wees worked on it together!

CHAPTER 2

The Pee Wees Throw Their Hats into the Ring

Roger began to pound the table. "We want our new badge," he chanted. "We want our new badge!"

Some of the other Pee Wees pounded the table too, and took up the chant.

"What is it? What is it?" asked Patty Baker. She was Kenny's twin sister.

"I hope it's not work," Sonny said through a yawn. "I hope it's just fun."

"It will be fun," said Mrs. Peters. "Loads and loads of fun."

The Pee Wees cheered. Fun was something none of them could get enough of.

Mrs. Peters held up her hand for silence.

"You've probably seen the campaign posters around town, in the stores, and on front lawns," she said.

Everyone stared at her. What did this have to do with badges? And fun? Campaign posters weren't fun. The Pee Wees couldn't vote.

"Elections are coming," their leader went on. "We live in a democracy, where we have a choice of who is in charge of our city and of our country."

Tim yawned. Roger made snoring noises. No one really wanted to hear about a democracy, thought Molly. They learned about stuff like that in school.

12

Mrs. Peters explained that some countries had kings who made the rules. The people had no say in their government. She talked about how lucky Americans were and how lucky the Pee Wees were to be able to grow up in a free country and vote.

"Our country isn't free," said Tim. "Everything costs money."

Rachel groaned. Mrs. Peters explained how *people* were free, not *things* in the stores.

Lisa waved her hand. "What about our badge?" she asked.

Mrs. Peters laughed. "I'm getting to that," she said. "Be patient."

That was what Molly's dad always said. Be patient. Molly hated to be patient. She hated to wait. It seemed as if waiting was all she ever did. Waiting for Christmas, waiting for her birthday, waiting for summer vacation, waiting for Mrs. Peters to tell them about their new badge.

Now Mrs. Peters was drawing something on the blackboard. Just like in school, thought Molly.

"This is a ballot box," said Mrs. Peters. "And this," she went on, "is a voting machine. On election day people go to the polls to cast their vote. They go behind a curtain and pull the lever for the man or woman they want to put in office. In small towns, they don't always have a machine. People may write the name of a candidate on a piece of paper and put their vote into a box."

"Where's the window?" Sonny asked.

"What window?" Mrs. Peters looked puzzled. "There is no window."

"You said there's a curtain," said Sonny.

Some of the other Pee Wees nodded.

"You did," said Patty. "You said they go behind a curtain."

"The curtain is in front of the voting machine," said Mrs. Peters. "It covers a little booth so that the person has privacy."

"Do people take off their clothes?" asked Tim. "Like in dressing rooms?"

"Of course not. Why would they do that?" asked their leader.

"Then why do they need privacy?" asked Tim.

Rachel groaned. "Because their vote is private," she said.

"That's right," said their leader. "Voting is a private choice."

"Yada yada yada," said Roger.

"He is so rude," said Tracy. "That's no way to talk to a Scout leader."

Mrs. Peters didn't seem to have heard Roger. She erased the voting machine and the ballot box and drew a town. There were hills and trees and houses and a post office. At least Molly thought it was a post office. It had a flag on it.

"This," said their leader when she'd finished, "is Peeweeville!"

Now all the Pee Wees were paying attention. What in the world was Peeweeville?

"What's Peeweeville?" asked Kenny.

"Peeweeville is an imaginary town where the Pee Wee Scouts run the city as the elected officials. There is a Pee Wee mayor, some Pee Wee councilpeople, a Pee Wee dogcatcher, a school superintendent, and a chief of police."

"Who are these Pee Wees?" shouted Tracy.

Mrs. Peters smiled. "You are!" she said. Everyone looked baffled.

"You are the Pee Wees who are going to

run for office! You are going to campaign and make posters and vote and choose the best person for the job. You are going to be mayor and councilpeople. You are going to run the town!"

Tim burst into tears. "I don't know how to be a mayor," he said.

"I do," said Kevin. "I'd like to run for mayor!"

"Well, this will be your big chance," said Mrs. Peters. "You may be elected mayor of Peeweeville."

"Do we have to run for office?" demanded Rachel. "I don't like politics much. I'm too busy. I take dance lessons on Thursday, and violin on Saturday, and—"

Mrs. Peters stopped her. "You have to campaign in order to get your new badge," she said. "But not everyone will be nominated, or elected, of course."

"What's nominated?" asked Sonny.

"That's when people decide who will run for office," said Jody. "It's when they choose the candidates."

Jody was so smart, thought Molly. He could run Peeweeville, or even Elm City, with one hand tied behind him, as her grandma liked to say. Molly would surely vote for Jody.

Mrs. Peters was busy telling everyone how to campaign. They had to say what office they wanted to run for. They had to make a list of what they would change in the city and what new laws they would make. They had to make campaign posters so that they would be noticed. They had to tell everyone why they would be the best candidate for the job.

"I don't want to be mayor," said Sonny.

"I want to be dogcatcher," said Lisa.

"I'm allergic to dogs," said Tracy.

"This is a dumb badge," said Sonny. "There's no Peeweeville anyway."

"I think Mrs. Peters's idea of fun is really work," Mary Beth whispered to Molly.

Rat's knees, thought Molly. She had a feeling her friend was right. A little while before, Molly had thought she didn't have to worry about voting because the Pee Wees were way too young.

Well, it seemed she was wrong. They were old enough to vote—*and* run for office.

CHAPTER 3

Work or Fun?

Before the meeting ended, Mrs. Peters passed out little booklets about cities and how they were run. She gave the Pee Wees pamphlets about voting. And she gave them flyers with pictures of the city officials in their town, and of the people who were really running for office. One of the people was Cliff Nelson.

"You can find out more about the issues on the Internet," she said. "And in the newspapers and at the library."

Molly didn't want to know more.

"This feels like school," grumbled Mary Beth. "Like we have to do a report or something."

"You have to know about cities in order to run one," said Mrs. Peters.

"She must have heard me," whispered Mary Beth, turning red.

"Once you decide what office you would like to run for," said Mrs. Peters, "let me know. Then you can make posters with your picture on it. You can think of a catchy saying that people will remember, like 'cleaner lakes' or 'better schools.' You can make flyers to pass out, telling what you will do if you're elected, just like the flyers I gave you."

"We'll set up a make-believe TV station, and each of you will have a chance to talk for a few moments and tell us what you'll do if you're elected. Then, on Election

Day, we all will actually vote and elect officials to run Peeweeville."

"Can we have debates?" asked Kevin. "I'd like to debate Jody on TV. Like the presidents do."

"If you like," said their leader. "But I think it will be enough work just to prepare a short talk."

There it was again, the word *work*, when Mrs. Peters had said the badge would be fun. But Kevin and Jody both loved work, and they always did a little extra to earn their badges. Work was the same as fun to them.

Sonny's mother, who was assistant Scout leader, brought in some pumpkin cookies with frosting and passed them around. Stuck in each cookie was a toothpick with a tiny American flag. This was a political treat, thought Molly.

The Pee Wees who had done good

deeds that week told about them (there were only three), and then they sang their Pee Wee song and said their pledge. The meeting was over. It was time to go.

"Rat's knees," said Molly to Mary Beth on the way home. "I don't know what I want to run for."

"I don't want to run for anything," said her best friend, kicking at some oak leaves. "I'll bet Kevin and Jody will run for mayor. Which one would you vote for?"

Molly wouldn't be able to make up her mind. She liked them both. They both were good at whatever they did. But a town couldn't have two mayors. It would be a hard choice.

"I'll have to wait and see what they say they'll do," said Molly wisely.

"That doesn't mean anything," scoffed

Mary Beth. "My dad says campaign promises are always broken."

"Kevin and Jody wouldn't lie!" said Molly, frowning. "They're both honest!"

Mary Beth shrugged. "Not when they run for office," she said. "These guys turn really mean. They say bad things about each other to get the vote."

Molly didn't believe this. At least about Kevin and Jody.

"Roger might do that," she said. "That's the only way he could get people to vote for him. But Kevin and Jody wouldn't."

"Ha!" said her friend. "Wait and see."

Roger came running up behind them. "I'm going to be mayor!" he shouted. "I want to be the biggest thing you can be in the city."

"The biggest fool," said Mary Beth. "No

one will vote for you. You don't even obey laws. Mayors always obey laws."

"Pooh," said Roger.

"Well, they should," said Mary Beth. "That's why we vote. To get someone better."

"Maybe I'll run for mayor," said Molly.

Roger looked shocked. "A girl mayor?" he shrieked. "No way!"

Mary Beth stamped her foot. "Girls can do anything boys can," she said. "In fact, I think Molly would make a great mayor."

"Boy, that won't be any competition for *me*!" said Roger. "I'll win in a minute! Nobody would vote for a girl."

Roger ran off laughing and shouting to catch his friends and tell them the silly news. "Molly for mayor—ha ha ha!"

"I don't know anything about being

mayor," said Molly, sounding worried about what she had said.

"Neither does he," Mary Beth said. "That doesn't matter. You can read about what to do and make better promises than he will."

Molly felt more worried now. She didn't want to be mayor. She just wanted to be sure Roger didn't get to be mayor. That was not a good reason for doing something.

Of course, Kevin and Jody would run, and they would get elected anyway. Even so, Molly had to keep her word. She had told two people that she would run for mayor, and now Roger was telling others. She didn't want to be a chicken.

"I could be your campaign manager," said Mary Beth. "Mayors need managers to help them make signs and stuff. I'll ask Mrs. Peters if it's okay. Then we could work twice as hard. I'll bet Roger won't have a manager."

When the girls got to Molly's house, Mary Beth went in with Molly.

"Molly's going to run for mayor," she said to the Duffs. "And I'm going to be her campaign manager!"

Well, now the news was really out. Molly had no choice. Mary Beth called Mrs. Peters to make sure she could manage Molly's campaign. When she hung up, she said, "Mrs. Peters said it was fine! And she said, " 'to the victor belong the spoils.' I wonder what that means?"

So did Molly.

CHAPTER 4

Molly for Mayor

All week long Molly and Mary Beth read about what a mayor did. They made big posters and lots of flyers. They thought up lots of campaign promises.

"The good thing about Peeweeville," said Mary Beth, "is that it isn't real. I mean, you don't actually have to keep your promises once you're elected. We'll just get the badge and forget all about it."

Molly didn't think that was a good spirit to have when she was running for mayor. She certainly wanted to keep the promises she made. Someday she might be a real mayor, and this would be good practice. Just in case.

"I think we should only make promises that are sensible," she said.

"You can bet Roger won't," said Mary Beth. "He'll say things like 'I'll build a new zoo' and 'I'll let all the prisoners out of jail.'"

"It would be awful to let all the prisoners out," said Molly.

"Of course, but Roger would do it, he's so dumb," said Mary Beth.

"I'll bet Jody and Kevin will have great promises," said Molly.

"Well, we'll know on Tuesday," said Mary Beth.

But when Tuesday came and they went to their meeting, the girls had a surprise. Jody was not running for mayor.

"I want to run for school superinten-dent," he said. "I think I could be more effective there."

Effective was a big word. Leave it to Jody to use it. He was so smart he should be president. Even the president didn't use words as big as Jody's.

"A lot of changes are needed in the schools," he said. "I think good teachers should get more money. Teachers are really important. Kids believe what they say."

How smart of Jody! Kevin would have a hard time winning against him!

But when Kevin came in, he was carry-ing a sign that said VOTE FOR KEVIN, THE COUNCILMAN FROM HEAVEN!

"I think I can be more effective on the city council," he said to the Pee Wees.

There was that word again!

"On the council I can be more in touch with the common people. I can work among them and get more done."

That sounded like something Molly's dad would say. Maybe Kevin's dad had said it! He was probably very smart too.

"Good for you, Kevin," said Mrs. Peters.

"With those guys out of the way, you have a great chance to really get elected!" said Mary Beth. "We'll have to work even harder!"

It was true. If Kevin and Jody weren't running for mayor, Molly would be Roger's toughest competition. It looked as if the only other Pee Wee running for mayor was Tim, and he was too quiet to be a good politician. At least that was what Mary Beth told Molly. "He hasn't got a chance," she said. "It's you or Roger."

"Rachel," said Mrs. Peters. "What will you run for?"

"I'm going to run for councilwoman," said Rachel, with a toss of her head.

"Fine," said their leader.

"I'd hate to be Kevin running against her," said Mary Beth. "Rachel is smart."

"So is Kevin," said Molly. "He can hold his own."

"We should really vote for Rachel," said Mary Beth. "We women have to stick together."

At the meeting, the Pee Wees worked on signs and posters. Mrs. Peters had lots of paper and paints and scissors.

Tim's sign said TIM FUR MARE.

Lisa's had a picture of a dog that looked more like a cat.

"Its legs are too short," said Mary Beth.

On the sign it said LET ME CATCH YOUR DOGS.

"I'm going to keep all the dogs I catch," said Lisa, "and have them for pets."

"You can't," Roger shouted. "That's against the law. They have to go to the dog pound and get made into glue."

The Pee Wees looked shocked.

Lisa added some words to her sign. They said I WON'T TURN YOUR DOGS INTO GLUE.

"They don't turn them into glue," said Jody. "If no one claims them they give them shots and find them good homes."

Kenny was running for dogcatcher too. His sign said SAVE OUR PETS.

Sonny was running against Jody. He made a big red sign that said SHORTER SCHOOL DAYS. NO HOMEWORK. LONGER VACATIONS.

"I don't care about that teachers' pay stuff," he said. "I'd do things for the kids, like longer recess and pizza every day."

"I want to be chief of police," said Tracy. "I'd like to drive one of those fast cars with the siren on and the red lights flashing."

"The chief doesn't drive around arresting people," said Kevin. "He stays in the office and makes sure all the police officers are doing good work."

"That's okay," said Tracy. "I wouldn't mind that. I could ride with them sometimes."

Patty was running against Tracy.

"Two girls for police chief!" yelled Sonny. "I want to be police chief! A girl can't do it!"

"You can't be police chief. You said you were running for school superintendent."

"I forgot about police chief! I want to be police chief!"

"Then Jody will win and get to make all the school rules," said Patty.

Now Sonny was worried. Jody wanted more pay for teachers, not pizza and recess.

"I want to run for both," he said.

"Only one office per Pee Wee," said Mrs. Peters firmly.

"Okay," grumbled Sonny. "I'll be the school boss."

"In your dreams," said Rachel.

By the time the meeting was over, everyone had signed up for something. Everyone had made a sign and some flyers.

Molly, Tim, and Roger were running for mayor.

Kenny and Lisa were running for dogcatcher.

Kevin and Rachel were running for councilperson.

Sonny and Jody were running for school superintendent.

Patty and Tracy were running for chief of police.

And everyone was sure they would win. Except Molly.

CHAPTER 5

Campaign Fever

"I'm going to put signs up in the grocery store and the bank and the drugstore," said Mary Beth. "That's what a good manager does. Gets you lots of attention. Maybe you could even get on TV like Cliff Nelson. He just smiles and holds his baby and says, 'I'm a family man.' "

"I wouldn't know what to say on TV," said Molly.

"We could find you a baby to hug," said Mary Beth. "All politicians hug babies. That gets votes."

How did Mary Beth know so much? Molly was lucky to have her for a manager.

Mary Beth had gone to the stores and bank and asked if she could put a sign in their windows.

"Everybody said yes, except old man Fogel, at the medical building. He doesn't let anyone hang up any signs. But that's okay because I have a better idea than signs," she said. "I think we should go to the mall and shake hands and kiss babies."

Molly was doubtful. Still, if her manager said to go to the mall, her manager knew best. After all, Mrs. Peters had been in favor of a campaign manager.

The girls told their mothers where they were going and started the short walk to the mall.

"I wish this was a big mall, one of those

huge ones where lots of people come," said Mary Beth, frowning. "This one's dinky."

Molly had to agree that their mall was small. It had only four stores. But it had a roof over it and a tree growing in the middle.

"Wait!" said Mary Beth, snapping her fingers. "We need to take a baby along to be a sample, in case there are no babies there."

She led the way to Sonny's house. Sonny had a little twin brother and sister. They were not tiny babies—they were big enough to go for a ride in a stroller.

Mary Beth knocked on the door. "Can we borrow your babies?" she asked Mrs. Stone politely. "We'd like to take them for a little walk, say, to the mall. It's such a nice day."

"Why do you want my babies?" shouted Sonny from inside the house.

The girls ignored him.

"Why, what a good idea!" said his mother. "I'll be glad to have some time to myself for an hour! And you two girls are so good with babies."

She bundled the twins up and put them in the double stroller. She told the girls to be careful crossing streets and to come back in an hour, and she shut the door.

"Why do you want my babies?" shouted Sonny from the window as they walked down the street.

The girls ignored him. When they got to the mall, Mary Beth put a big sign in front of Molly that said MOLLY FOR MAYOR OF PEEWEEVILLE.

"Now if a real baby comes along, you can kiss it—if the mother doesn't mind," she said. "But if a grown-up comes along without a baby, you shake their hand and say, 'I hope I have your vote,' then kiss one of our own babies here."

The Stone twins were busy sucking their pacifiers and watching the girls. It was very quiet in the mall. Hardly any people were there. Elm City was a small town. Most people shopped on weekends. Often they went to the big stores in Minneapolis.

"You can practice kissing these kids," said Mary Beth. "Go ahead. Just on the top of their heads."

Molly felt silly, but a campaign manager was a campaign manager. Mary Beth knew more than Molly about what would get votes.

Finally a man came by and stopped. "I hope I have your vote, sir," said Molly.

He looked surprised.

"When is the election?" he asked.

"A week from Tuesday," said Mary Beth. "At our Scout meeting at Mrs. Peters's house."

"I'll be out of town," the man said.

Mary Beth whipped a paper out of her pocket. "Here is an absentee ballot," she said. "You can fill in the names and send it in."

"Who else is running?" he asked.

"Tim Noon and Roger White," said Mary Beth. "And you wouldn't want either one of them. Trust me. They're not mayor material."

The man walked away, shaking his head.

"I just thought of something," said Molly. "It's really the Pee Wee votes we need. I mean, Mrs. Peters may not let strangers come to the meeting and vote."

Mary Beth looked thoughtful. "She said Tuesday was voting day. I'm sure that means anyone. I mean, this is a democracy."

Molly shook her head. "If that was true, Rachel could get all her dad's patients to vote, and you'd get all your aunts and uncles, and my mom could get people from work. I don't think grown-ups can vote. It's just the Pee Wees that vote in this election."

"Rat's knees!" said Mary Beth, using Molly's favorite saying. "That means all this hand shaking and baby kissing is for nothing! We need to get the Pee Wees out here!"

But there were no Pee Wees in the mall.

"Maybe we should go where they are, like the park," said Molly.

Mary Beth was playing peekaboo with the twins. They began to giggle.

"Babies are fun, aren't they?" she said. Then she stood up. "Okay, let's go to the park."

She took the sign down, and Molly pushed the stroller.

"The hour's almost up. We'd better get these kids home," said Molly.

As they got to Sonny's house, he was glaring out the window, making ugly faces.

"Your face might freeze that way," shouted Mary Beth.

Mrs. Stone thanked the girls and said they could take the twins for a walk anytime.

Mary Beth ran to her house and got some flyers they had made, and the girls headed for the park. Sure enough, several of the Pee Wees were there, playing on the swings and slides and jungle bars. Mary Beth led Molly to the middle of the park where everyone could see them. She set up the big sign. Then she began to hand out the flyers to the Pee Wees.

"Molly is the best bet," she called to them. "If you don't vote for her, you're all wet!"

Molly smiled and tried to shake the Pee Wees' hands, but none of them except Tim and Jody wanted to shake hers.

"That's not fair," said Roger. "Advertising isn't fair."

"Why not? You could advertise if you wanted to," said Molly. "What you need is a campaign manager."

"Do not," said Roger.

"Do too," said Mary Beth.

Suddenly Roger got on his bike and left. "See? We scared him away. We're so good at campaigning," Mary Beth said. "We have what they call campaign fever.

"Here she is!" she shouted. "The mayor that's a whiz! Vote for Molly, by golly!"

Molly didn't know about the fever, but she knew she wanted to win!

CHAPTER 6

Mudslinging

In half an hour Roger was back with American flags and posters. He had a boom box that blared "My Country, 'Tis of Thee," and he stood on a stool waving a banner that said NO GIRL FOR MAYOR! A MAN IS NEEDED FOR THIS JOB!

"Ha!" said Rachel. "Where's the man, Roger? It's sure not you!"

Roger stuck out his tongue at Rachel and made a face.

"We should take his picture," said Ra-

chel. "A mayor sticking out his tongue? I don't think so!"

"That would be blackmail," said Mary Beth. "It's not allowed. You have to fight fair and square."

"Roger isn't!" said Lisa. "Listen to all the bad things he's saying about Molly! Just because she's a girl!"

Sure enough, Roger was screaming above the music: "Keep Molly out! Keep Molly out! No girl for mayor! No girl for mayor!

"A vote for me is a vote for TV," he went on. "I'll make sure every Pee Wee has their own TV in their bedroom. I'll make parents let kids stay up as late as they want. And I'll build some more city swimming pools right near our houses."

"Jody already has a pool," said Patty. "And we always go to Tiger Lake. We don't need any more pools."

All the Pee Wees were listening to Roger now instead of to Molly. It wouldn't have mattered how many babies she hugged. Roger was getting all the attention. He was making a lot more noise.

" 'The squeaky wheel gets the grease,' " declared Mary Beth. "That's what my grandma says."

Molly didn't know what a squeaky wheel had to do with Roger, but before she could ask, Mary Beth explained, "The one who talks the loudest gets the vote."

As the girls watched, Roger opened his backpack and took out a sack of candy bars. He held them up and said, "For every vote, you get a candy bar!" And all the Pee Wees except Jody and Kevin and Rachel swarmed over to collect. Even Mary Beth!

"Get back here!" shrieked Molly. "You're voting for *me*!"

"I love those caramel clusters," Mary Beth said.

"Rat's knees!" said Molly. "Roger is turning out to be a better manager than you!"

Mary Beth looked sheepish. Their sign looked pretty mild now. Roger was beating a drum and singing, "Beat Molly! Beat Molly! Beat Molly!" and "My candy is dandy! My candy is dandy!" And the other Scouts were chanting along with him!

Tim was sitting on a park bench eating one of Roger's candy bars and wearing a sign saying VOTE FER ME.

"You have to vote for Roger now, you know, since you took a candy bar," said Lisa.

"Do not," said Tim. "He said I do, but I'm not going to."

Tim was smarter than Molly had

thought! Roger was playing dirty, and Tim knew it! Maybe they all would take his candy bars but vote for Molly because she had such a good campaign.

"Roger is a mudslinger," said Mary Beth. "My dad said never to throw mud. That means saying bad stuff about the other candidate."

"Unless you sling mud too, to get back at him," said Rachel. "You could make signs saying 'Roger's a dummy; as mayor he'd be crummy,' or something."

Molly and Mary Beth thought about it.

"I think we'll win by being better than he is. We don't have to stoop to dirty tricks," said Mary Beth.

Rat's knees, Molly thought. Was Mary Beth right? Or would Roger's tricks work? Maybe Molly should throw mud after all! Being a good guy didn't always work. What did they say on TV? "Good guys finish last." Molly didn't want to finish last!

Now Mary Beth turned their sign over and wrote in black letters WE DON'T SLING MUD. WE PLAY CLEAN. WE WILL CLEAN UP CITY HALL. WE ARE FAIR TO EVERYONE. She walked around the park holding up the sign.

No one paid much attention.

Now some of the other Pee Wees were campaigning too. Jody's wheelchair had flags and streamers on it. On the back was a red, white, and blue sign that read DON'T BE A MULE, VOTE FOR GOOD SCHOOLS. VOTE JODY GEORGE!

Soon it seemed all the Pee Wees were in the park. Lisa was pulling a wagon with a puppy and kitten in it. They had green bows around their necks. On the side of the wagon it said I'LL PICK UP YOUR PET, AND TAKE IT TO THE VET!

"She's supposed to take it to the dog

pound," said Kenny. "That's what I'd do if I was elected."

Sonny held a paper flag that said MORE RECESS, MORE VACATION, MORE PIZZA.

Rachel had taken her tap shoes out of a bag and was doing a dance. She turned cartwheels and somersaults on the lawn and sang some words to the tune of "Three Blind Mice":

Tap, tap, tap. See how I run.
I'll dance right into the council room.
I'll get the work done with a zoom
    zoom zoom.
I'll get it all done before noon, noon,
    noon.
I'll beat Kevin Moe.

"That's what we should have done!" said Mary Beth. "A dance! That's a good way to get votes. People like entertainment."

It was true. All eyes were on Rachel and her acrobatics. Her act was as popular as Roger's candy bars.

And all Molly had was a dull, quiet sign.

CHAPTER 7

High and Mighty

"**B**ut I can't dance!" Molly told Mary Beth.

Mary Beth sighed. "We need something that gets more attention. We'd better call a meeting."

"Who of?" asked Molly.

"The candidate and her manager," said Mary Beth.

"That's us," said Molly. "We're already meeting."

"Not officially," said Mary Beth. "We have to have a real meeting, like at a table or desk, and talk about new strategies. It's called brainstorming."

Kevin was playing a trumpet now.

Tracy was riding her little brother's tricycle. She'd put a box around it painted to look like a police car. It had a noisy siren on the handlebar. It got attention.

Patty had turned her bike into a police motorcycle. She wore a homemade police uniform, with a helmet and goggles.

Tim was the only one who wasn't doing anything. He sat with his sign and watched.

"The sooner we brainstorm the better," said Molly. "These Pee Wees know how to campaign."

The girls took their sign and went to Molly's house.

"Let's go in the garage where we can be alone," said Mary Beth. "It will be more official."

The garage smelled like gas and oil and paint, thought Molly. Not like a meeting room. There was no table or desk, so the girls sat in folding lawn chairs.

"Now," said Mary Beth, "I'm calling this meeting to order. You have to second the motion."

Molly did.

And then there didn't seem to be anything to say.

"Think," said Mary Beth. "Think hard about what we can do to win."

Molly frowned so that she would look as if she were thinking. But her mind was blank.

"Let's think about what the real candidates do to get votes," said Mary Beth.

"They go on TV," said Molly. "And take out big ads in the paper."

Mary Beth thought about that. "We can't afford TV," she said. "Or newspaper ads. They cost a lot of money, especially big ones. When I put an ad in the paper to sell my skates, it cost five dollars."

Molly whistled. That was a lot of money. The Pee Wees didn't have that much money.

"What can we do that's free?" asked Mary Beth.

Free was harder. Free didn't give them many choices.

"I think I have it!" said Mary Beth suddenly. "You know those planes that write words in the air in smoke? We can ask them to write 'Molly for mayor' in the clouds!"

Mary Beth was turning out to be a bad manager, thought Molly.

"We don't even know a pilot," she said. "Besides, pilots are too busy flying those great big planes with hundreds of people on them to France or somewhere. They wouldn't bother to write my name in smoke."

"Let's keep thinking," said Mary Beth. "We have to come up with something. 'Where there's a will there's a way,' my aunt says."

Mary Beth's whole family was full of sayings. Molly wasn't sure about any of them.

"Of course, the idea of putting something up in the air is a good one," said Mary Beth thoughtfully. "I mean, everyone would see it. Like putting a sign on top of the bank building. It's about umpteen stories high."

"How would we get a sign up there?" asked Molly. "Even if we got to the top floor we couldn't crawl out a window that high up. Anyway, I bet all the windows are locked. And what would we tie it to? Even duct tape wouldn't hold for one minute in that wind."

Molly was upset that she had to be the voice of reason. What was Mary Beth thinking?

"Well, we're just brainstorming," said her friend, who seemed to know what Molly was thinking. "That's what business guys do."

"I suppose we could go up to my uncle's apartment," Mary Beth went on. "He lives on the tenth floor, and he has a little balcony with plants and stuff on it. He says I can come up anytime. He gave us a key."

"Maybe," said Molly, "instead of a sign we could drop something saying 'Vote for Molly' on it."

Mary Beth got out of her lawn chair so fast it tipped over. She snapped her fin-

gers and said, "That's it! That's the idea we needed! We'll drop balloons from the balcony! You see how well brainstorming works? I move we adjourn this meeting and go and get balloons!"

"I second the motion," said Molly.

Mary Beth wrote something down in her notebook.

Then she said, "It has been moved and seconded that we adjourn this meeting, since we have a good idea about balloons."

Mary Beth took a hammer from the workbench and pounded it on the arm of Molly's chair. "The meeting is ended," she said.

"Where do we get the balloons?" asked Molly.

"I think I have some left over from my sister's party," said her friend.

"We need a lot," said Molly.

The girls ran to Mary Beth's house. In the basement were six balloons, all in the air with strings hanging from them. They were big and puffy and silver. They all said HAPPY BIRTHDAY.

"We'll just cross that out and write 'Vote for Molly' instead," said Mary Beth. "And we can write on the other side too. Silver will catch the light and sparkle. Everyone will notice them."

Mary Beth got some colored markers. The girls worked and worked, crossing off HAPPY BIRTHDAY and writing VOTE FOR MOLLY on every balloon twice. That made twelve signs.

"We really need more than this," said Molly. "But at least it's a start. Let's get over to your uncle's."

"I have to ask my mom for the key," said Mary Beth.

But Mary Beth's mother was not home.

A note said, "At the dentist. Back in an hour."

"I know where the key is," said Mary Beth. "I'll be right back."

She ran to the kitchen and grabbed the key, and off they went.

When they arrived, the guard recognized Mary Beth. He said, "Hi there. Go right up." He looked at all the balloons. "Is it your uncle's birthday?"

"Not today," she replied, "but pretty soon!"

Her uncle was not at home. The girls struggled with the lock until finally the key turned. They stopped to pet Rollie, the cat, and then went out on the balcony.

"Boy, are we ever high!" said Molly. "You can see the whole town from here!"

"Let's just drop these over the edge so we can leave," said Mary Beth.

Molly did. But she was in for a surprise!

The balloons did not drop. They did not fall to the ground advertising Molly's name. Instead, they went up up up in the air, higher and higher. Past the eleventh floor. Past the roof. Far too high for anyone to read unless they were a bird or in an airplane!

"Helium!" said Mary Beth, stamping her foot. "Those balloons have helium in them. They're gone for good!"

CHAPTER 8

Up in the Air

"**W**hy didn't you think of that?" demanded Molly. "You're my manager."

"Me?" said Mary Beth. "You could have thought of it, too, you know."

Molly sighed. "Well, there's nothing to be done except to get packages of regular balloons and blow them up. Balloons without helium."

The girls locked up the apartment and went home to get money from their banks for more balloons. They bought two packages at the drugstore. Then they sat in

Molly's backyard and blew them up. They wrote the same words on the balloons all over again. Then they tied them together with string so that they could carry them to the balcony.

The guard was busy talking to a man in a uniform and just waved them on in. When they got to the tenth floor, they let themselves in with the key.

"I'm tired!" said Molly, falling onto the couch. "This campaigning is very hard work!"

"You know," said Mary Beth, looking down at the trees and city, "these balloons may not fall because they're too light. They need something heavy in them."

"We don't have rocks," said Molly.

They both thought of a solution at the same time! "Water!" said Mary Beth.

Molly untied the balloons, and Mary Beth filled them with water at the sink.

Then she tied them up again and dropped each one over the edge of the balcony. This time the girls were successful. One by one the balloons dropped to the ground.

"I hope Roger is watching," said Molly. "And the other Pee Wees. I hope they see how we are doing the best campaigning of all!"

"The balloons are falling near the park," said Mary Beth. "I don't see how they can miss them."

"Maybe one will fall on Roger's head!" laughed Molly. "That would serve him right. *Splash!*"

"I just know you're going to win," said Mary Beth. "This is a great strategy."

Molly wasn't sure what strategy was, but if it helped her win against Roger, she was all for it.

The girls locked the door and left the building. Mary Beth said, "We have to start thinking of a victory song. I could make up new words for a song we sing at football games."

She sat down on Molly's front steps and took out her notebook.

"We can sing 'Molly, Molly, hats off to thee, firm and strong in victory, rah rah for Molly Duff!' "

The girls sang it together. Then they walked to the park singing.

"I don't see any of our balloons!" said Mary Beth. "But they must have landed down here somewhere."

As they walked, they saw some little puddles. In the middle of the puddles were little pieces of rubber.

"The balloons broke when they hit the ground!" said Molly. "Look! Some of them hit a sharp rock or a branch. All the balloons popped!"

Mary Beth stamped her foot. "Rat's

knees!" she said. "All our work for nothing."

At the park Rachel was still doing cartwheels.

Roger was giving out packages of gum.

"That's bad for your teeth," said Molly.

"It's sugarless," said Roger.

Rat's knees! Roger thought of everything! *He* should have been her campaign manager!

"Why is your hair all wet?" demanded Mary Beth.

"Some dumb balloon hit me on the head and it was filled with water. Who would do a dumb thing like that?" Roger said.

Mary Beth poked her friend and giggled. "Well, at least our idea made one good thing happen!" she said.

Mrs. Peters came through the park, pushing baby Nick in his stroller.

"Who are you going to vote for?" Rachel asked her.

"Oh no, I'm not telling!" said their leader. "But I'm sure the best person will win!"

She waved to the Pee Wees and walked on.

"Well, she didn't take any of Roger's candy or gum," said Mary Beth.

"That's because she's nonpartisan," said Rachel.

"Why doesn't she like Parmesan?" asked Tim. "It's really good on spaghetti."

Rachel groaned. "Nonpartisan means she isn't for one side or another."

"Next Tuesday we vote," said Molly. "And I don't think I have a chance against those candy bars and gum."

"Anyone can see that you're better material than Roger," Mary Beth said.

She makes it sound as if I was cut out of a piece of cloth, thought Molly.

"We're running a cleaner campaign and making sensible promises," Mary Beth added. "The Pee Wees will know you're trustworthy. Roger doesn't stand a chance."

But Molly was not too sure. People might remember candy much longer than they'd remember how dumb and selfish Roger was. Or what a good mayor Molly would make.

She wouldn't have to wait long to find out.

Tuesday would be here before they knew it!

CHAPTER 9

The Washable Ad!

"**W**e have to have a big push before the election," said Mary Beth.

"What do you mean?" asked Molly.

"A last-minute campaign thing," said Mary Beth. "You know, do something to make voters remember you at the polls. Something spectacular!"

"Like what?" asked Molly. "We did everything we could think of to get votes. But Roger is going to win." She looked sad.

Mary Beth shook her head. "It's not too late until the last vote is in," she said.

Molly felt as if it were too late, but she was glad her friend was hopeful.

"Let's see," said Mary Beth. "What could we do? I wish we had a great idea!"

Just then a car drove by slowly. Tin cans were tied to the bumper, making a lot of noise. When people looked to see what was making the noise, they noticed words painted on the sides of the car.

"It's like a wedding," scoffed Mary Beth, "when they say 'Just Married'."

These words did not say JUST MARRIED. They said ROGER MOE'S THE MAN FOR THE JOB!

"Rat's knees!" said Molly. "That's Mr. Moe's car! He painted his sign right on the car! He must be really anxious for Roger to win, if he'd ruin his car!"

"That's just washable paint," said Mary

Beth. "It will come off when it rains. I wish we'd thought of that. Roger's name will really stick in their minds."

"Rat's knees, we can still do that," said Molly. "Our dads have cars!"

"We could," said Mary Beth thoughtfully. "I mean, he doesn't own the idea or anything."

The girls ran to Mary Beth's house. Her dad was in the garage. Mary Beth ran to ask him. Molly saw him frown and shake his head.

"He said no," Mary Beth reported. "He doesn't like the idea. But what about your car?" she asked. "I mean, you're the one who's running for mayor. Your dad would be proud, I'll bet."

"I suppose I could ask," said Molly.

Mary Beth waved her hand, dismissing the idea of asking. "We don't need to ask," she said. "I mean, it's washable paint. I'll bet he wouldn't care at all. I'll bet he'd be proud!"

Molly wondered if her friend was right. Would her dad be proud? Mary Beth was already racing toward the Duffs' house.

"You have some of that housepaint in the basement!" she said. "I saw it. It says 'water base' on it—'Clean up with water.' That means it washes right off your hands and clothes. My uncle washes his brushes out with water—that's how I know."

If Mary Beth said it was washable, she must be right. She knew a lot. She hardly ever made mistakes.

The girls found the paint in the basement. "Maybe I should ask," said Molly.

But her parents had left a note saying they'd gone over to Molly's aunt's.

"We have no time to lose," said Mary

Beth. "We can't sit around waiting while we lose votes."

Now Mary Beth was prying the lid off the paint can. She stirred the paint with a stick.

"This is nice and bright," she said. "It will really get attention."

But when the girls got to the garage, the car was gone. Molly's parents had driven to her aunt's.

Mary Beth snapped her fingers. "I have a better idea!" she said. "Let's paint words across the front of your house instead! Then everyone in town can see it when they drive by! That will be even better than a sign on the car. And Roger can't say we copied him!"

"Are you sure the paint will wash off when it rains?" asked Molly.

"Pooh," said Mary Beth. "Of course.

Look what it says on the can: 'Easy cleanup. Wash brushes with water.' If it comes off brushes with water, it comes off other stuff."

Mary Beth dipped the brush in the paint and stood on her toes to paint the *M* for *Molly* under the porch windows. It was as high as she could reach. Molly had to admit it looked showy. It would get votes! Molly picked up another brush and helped her. They worked hard and soon it said "Molly for Mayor" all the way across her house.

"Now we'll just wash up with the hose," said Mary Beth.

The paint did wash out of the brushes with the water. And off the girls' hands.

"Like magic!" said Mary Beth. "It's only oil paint that's hard to get off."

"Let's sit on the steps and watch people read our sign," said Molly.

They sat on the steps for a half hour. Finally some cars came by and the people looked. Then they stared. One woman said, "Oh my!" and covered her mouth with her hand as if she was upset.

"She'll tell everyone, and the Pee Wees will all come to see," said Mary Beth.

Some people on the street walked by and stopped. They didn't say anything. They looked at the words and then walked on.

Another man came by, muttered, "Graffiti," and walked on.

"What's graffiti?" asked Mary Beth.

"Maybe it's like spaghetti," Molly said.

"Maybe he remembered he had to get some at the store on the way home," said Mary Beth.

Soon Rachel came along on her bike.

The girls waved. "Look!" they shouted. Rachel looked. She leaned her bike on a tree and came and sat down on the steps.

"Do your parents know you did this?" she demanded.

"What's the difference?" said Mary Beth. "It washes off."

Rachel went up and put her finger on the paint. "Not anymore," she said. "It's dry."

Rachel was smart, Molly knew, but not about everything. She must not know about paint, thought Molly. She was better at things like dancing and music.

Kevin came by, walking his dog.

"What did you guys do?" he shrieked.

Rachel told him.

"It's washable," said Molly. "My parents won't care."

"We washed the brushes out, clean as can be," said Mary Beth.

Kevin whistled a long, low whistle. "It's not washable once it dries," he said. "That stuff is on there for life!"

CHAPTER 10

The Big Mistake

"I told them that!" said Rachel, waving her arms. "Wait till your parents see this," she said.

Molly felt like crying. What had she done to her house? Would she have to live in a house all her life, all through high school and college, that said "Molly for Mayor" on it? Every time they took pictures of birthday parties or Fourth of July parties or Christmas parties in the front yard, it would say MOLLY FOR MAYOR in the picture! Even when she was an old lady!

Molly might doubt Rachel, but she knew Kevin wouldn't make a mistake like this. This was for real! Rat's knees, this was huge bad news! Worse than losing the election!

Kevin scratched at the paint. It didn't come off. It was stuck on tight.

"How could housepaint wash off?" asked Rachel. "If it washed off, all the houses would be bare when it rained!"

Why hadn't Molly and Mary Beth thought of that?

"I'd probably better go home," said Mary Beth. "I think it's time for supper."

Mary Beth left, and so did Kevin and Rachel.

"Good luck," called Kevin, shaking his head.

I'll need good luck, thought Molly. She tried to scrape the paint off with a stick, but it didn't budge. What would her mom

and dad say? What would they do? Molly was starting to cry when a car drove up. Her parents were back!

"Hi, Molly, how are—" her dad began to say. Then he saw the house. His mouth fell open and he got out of the car and stared. Her mother was speechless. She looked as if she might start crying.

"Who did this?" her dad asked.

"We thought it would come off," cried Molly. "It said *washable* on the paint can."

Molly's dad was quiet for a moment. Then he told Molly to go to her room. This was not a good sign. She hadn't eaten dinner yet.

Molly could hear her parents talking in the living room. She heard words like "Punishment" and "What was she thinking of?"

After what seemed like ages, there was

a knock on her bedroom door. Her parents came in. They did not look happy.

"This is very serious," said her dad, who usually laughed and teased Molly. He was not in a teasing mood now. He'll probably never tease me again, Molly thought.

"I'm sorry," Molly cried. "We never thought—"

"That's just it," said her mother. "You didn't think."

The phone rang. Molly heard her dad talking.

When he hung up he said, "That was Mr. Kelly. Mary Beth told him the whole story. He said he'll help repaint the house."

The house would have to be repainted! Molly knew that would be a lot of work.

Molly's dad talked to her for a long time about how she should ask before acting. He told her how expensive paint was, and what a big job it was to repaint a house.

"I'm sorry," said Molly. "I'll ask before I do anything. And I won't listen to Mary Beth ever again."

Her mom laughed. "You can listen," she said. "But ask us before you do anything rash."

Molly wasn't sure what *rash* was, but she was glad to see her mom laugh again. They still loved her! They would paint the house and fix the mistake. And Molly would never make such a big mistake again. At least she hoped she wouldn't.

The next weekend Mr. Kelly and Mr. Duff sanded the front of the Duffs' house. Molly and Mary Beth helped. The neighbors and Pee Wees watched.

"At least this is good publicity," said

Mary Beth as they sanded away. "This will make people remember Molly Duff."

"It's a pretty hard way to get votes," said Molly, whose arms were beginning to get stiff from the work.

On Tuesday the girls met Roger on the way to the Scout meeting. "What a dumb idea," he said. "You guys were really nutzo, do you know that?"

Molly paid no attention to Roger. And no one else mentioned the incident.

The Pee Wees all gathered around the big table in Mrs. Peters's basement. There were flags everywhere and signs saying VOTE HERE!

"Well, today is the big day!" said their leader. "We'll find out who the new officials of Peeweeville are! You've done a wonderful job campaigning, and now all the work is over and we'll see who ran the best campaigns! Today we vote."

Mrs. Peters passed out slips of paper.

"The names of all the nominees are on each ballot," she said. "You vote for just one candidate for each office by checking the box next to their name. Give your decision a lot of thought; don't hurry with your voting. Choose the person you think can do the job best. The laundry room is the voting booth, and we'll take turns just as at the real polls."

Mrs. Peters opened the door to the laundry room. There was a place to write on top of the dryer and a box on top of the washing machine. The box had a slot in the top.

"You mark your ballot and drop your vote in the ballot box."

"Do we put our own name on them?" asked Tracy.

"Of course not, silly," said Rachel. "No one is supposed to know who you voted for."

"That's right," said their leader. "This is a secret ballot."

"I could tell by the handwriting whose vote it is," said Mary Beth. "I mean, Tim writes real messy and he spells wrong."

"The names are already on the papers," Mrs. Peters reminded her. "You just put a check in the box after the name you choose."

The Pee Wees studied the paper. One by one they went into the laundry room. Most of them thought about their votes a long time. But Tim didn't. He went in, made some checks on the paper, and came right out.

"Roger is trying to see what I'm writing, Mrs. Peters!" said Rachel. "That's illegal. He's breaking the law."

Mrs. Peters glared at Roger. "Come back from the door," she said. "Don't try to peek."

Molly wondered if it was illegal to vote for herself. She was sure presidents did. They wouldn't vote for the other guy. And she surely didn't want to vote for Roger or Tim.

Finally only Jody still had to vote. Jody was last, Molly guessed, because he was the most thoughtful. He wouldn't rush into something so important.

When everyone had voted, they all sat down at the table. Mrs. Peters gave each Scout a cookie in the shape of a flag. It was red, white, and blue and had candy stars on it.

And now, at last, it was time to count the votes and announce the winners!

CHAPTER 11

The Winners Are . . . !

Mrs. Stone came down the steps to help Mrs. Peters count the votes. They went into the laundry room.

Meanwhile the Pee Wees argued about who would win.

"I hope Roger isn't mayor," said Rachel. "That would be a disaster."

"My mom says a lot of times the wrong person wins," said Tracy.

"A lot of people don't keep the promises they make," said Lisa. "So you have to wait for the next election and vote for someone else."

At last Mrs. Peters and Mrs. Stone came out of the laundry room. They put up a sign with all the candidates' names on it. Mrs. Peters started to write. After each name, she listed the number of votes the candidate got. The Pee Wees waited breathlessly.

"What if there's a tie?" asked Kenny. "Who would win then?"

"There can't be a tie," said Mrs. Stone. "With Mrs. Peters's, there are thirteen votes. With an uneven number of votes, there cannot be a tie."

"Good," said Rachel. "I'd hate to share the job of councilperson with Kevin."

"Well, I'm not going to share the mayor's job with anyone!" boasted Roger.

"You'll only be mayor in your dreams," said Mary Beth.

"I won!" said Lisa, jumping out of her chair when the dogcatcher's votes went up. "Kenny got six votes, and I got seven!"

Kenny was a good loser. He shook hands with Lisa and congratulated her.

"It was close," he said. "But you put up a good fight."

"That's really cool," said Rachel. "Kenny is so professional."

But when the votes for councilperson went up, Kevin had eight votes and Rachel had five.

"What?" shouted Rachel. "I worked harder than he did, campaigning! I demand a recount!"

She stamped her foot and looked as if she might cry. She was definitely not as cool as she'd said Kenny was.

"I think we have to take some time here to talk about being good losers," said Mrs.

Peters. "Only one person can win in each category. And the best lesson we can learn from this experience is how to be a graceful loser."

" 'It's not whether you win or lose,' " said Patty. " 'It's how you play the game.' My grandma says that."

"And it's true," said Mrs. Peters, looking at Rachel, who was now sobbing. "No one likes to lose, but losers have a chance to be more courageous than the winners."

Now Rachel sobbed harder.

"Nobody likes a sore loser," said Roger.

"Ha," said Mary Beth to Molly. "Let's see how he likes it when you win!"

Mrs. Peters posted the rest of the winners on the sign. Jody was elected school superintendent over Sonny, eleven votes to two.

"I'll bet everyone voted for Jody except Sonny and Roger!" shouted Tracy.

"Booo," yelled Sonny. "I demand a recount too."

"You don't need a recount," said Patty. "You lost."

Sonny began to sulk.

Patty won the office of chief of police over Tracy, eight votes to four. But Tracy was a good loser and shook Patty's hand. "My allergies would probably act up anyway," she said. "Police work is hard on the nerves."

There was only one office left. It was the office of mayor!

Slowly—very slowly, Molly thought—Mrs. Peters wrote the three remaining names on the board. She wrote numbers after them.

Roger: 1

Molly: 5

Tim: 7!!!

The Pee Wees all stared at the numbers.

Mary Beth waved her hand. "You made a mistake, Mrs. Peters," she said. "That should be Molly seven and Tim five. You just got them mixed up."

But their leader had not made a mistake. Tim was the new mayor of Peeweeville!

"How could that happen?" demanded Rachel, who had stopped crying. "It doesn't make sense."

"That's what's exciting about elections," said Jody. "They're full of surprises. No one knows till the votes are in what will happen."

"But Tim didn't even campaign," said Kenny.

"He can't even spell!" said Tracy.

Everyone stared at Tim. He was beaming. Mrs. Peters pinned a big red badge on Tim. It was not a Pee Wee badge. It was a badge that said MAYOR OF PEEWEEVILLE!

The other winners got badges too.

And then the Pee Wees celebrated with an election party. There were red, white, and blue balloons and streamers. There were fruit punch and cupcakes. The winners each came up front and took a bow. Tim looked very proud. "I knew I'd win," he said.

"How could he know that?" said Rachel. "Unless the voting was rigged."

After the election party, Mrs. Peters passed out the new Scout badges. They were red, white, and blue and had the word VOTE on them.

Molly was glad to have her new badge, but she would have been gladder if she had been the new mayor. She wished she was wearing Tim's red badge.

"You ruined your house and lost anyway," scoffed Sonny to Molly.

"So? You lost too," said Mary Beth.

"But I didn't do anything as dumb as painting my house," said Sonny. "I know better than that."

"You just didn't think of it," said Mary Beth.

The Pee Wees sang their song and said their pledge. Then they left for home.

On the way, Mary Beth and Molly talked about the election.

"How could Tim have won?" asked Mary Beth, stamping her foot on the sidewalk. "I mean, the one vote for Roger was probably Roger's. And we know five people voted for you. But who are the seven who voted for Tim?"

"Tim is one," said Molly. "And maybe Mrs. Peters felt sorry for him and thought he'd lose. So she wanted him to have at least one vote."

"Maybe Jody and Kevin felt sorry for him too, and thought they would give him one vote," said Mary Beth. "Those are called pity votes, you know."

"If they did, that's four, but what about the rest?"

Mary Beth turned red. "I voted for him too," she confessed. "But I thought mine would be the only vote he'd get and I'd make him feel good!"

Now it was Molly who stamped her foot. "You're my campaign manager!" she said. "The least you could have done was vote for me!"

Mary Beth looked sheepish. "I thought you'd win for sure without my vote. Anyway, that's only five," she said. "What about the two others?"

Now it was Molly's turn to blush and confess. "I voted for Tim too," she said. "It was a pity vote. There's still one vote more, though. Whose was that? Vote number seven?"

Mary Beth sighed. "I guess we'll never know," she said. "It's a secret vote. There's no way we can find out whose it was. It's the American way. It's democratic, you know."

"Rat's knees," said Molly. "Tim is mayor."

Molly remembered how pleased Tim had been. He never won games or prizes. He was so proud of being elected. He would definitely be a better mayor than Roger anyway.

"I think I'm glad he won," sighed Molly.

"So am I," said Mary Beth. "Race you to the corner!"

But Molly wasn't in the mood for any more races.

She'd let her campaign manager win this one.

Pee Wee Scout Song

(to the tune of
"Old MacDonald Had a Farm")

Scouts are helpers, Scouts have fun
Pee Wee, Pee Wee Scouts!
We sing and play when work is done,
Pee Wee, Pee Wee Scouts!
With a good deed here,
And an errand there,
Here a hand, there a hand,
Everywhere a good hand.

Scouts are helpers, Scouts have fun
Pee Wee, Pee Wee Scouts!

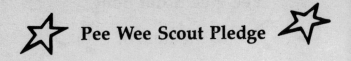 ## Pee Wee Scout Pledge

We love our country
And our home,
Our school and neighbors too.

As Pee Wee Scouts
We pledge our best
In everything we do.